Summer Nights

J.M. GOODRICH

Summer Nights

Copyright © 2022 J.M. Goodrich

About The Author

J.M. Goodrich is a native of Michigan's beautiful upper peninsula. She loves spending time outdoors as much as she can with her family when she's not reading or writing. She has been published in several different anthologies and novels of her own. She has written stories of romance, fantasy, and horror. In addition to her love of writing, she has a passion for music, and an obsession with The Beatles.

One

THE FRONT DOOR flew open with so much force it banged against the wall. Normally Ally was careful about the noise she made and was considerate of her neighbors, but today she's just about had it. With pretty much everything. She had just come from work where, yet again, she was passed by on a promised promotion. It instead had gone to a male coworker of hers with less than half her experience. It had been this way for years.

In her frustration she hadn't noticed her roommate sitting on the couch. Ally threw her purse in that direction, smacking her friend in the arm with it.

"Ouch," Stephanie exclaimed, rubbing the sore spot on her arm.

"Oh, my gosh, I am so sorry!" Ally exclaimed,

coming to sit next to her friend. "I didn't see you there. I feel so bad now."

Stephanie just laughed, shaking her head. "It's all right, it didn't hurt." She shifted in her seat. "Is everything okay though? You seem much more stressed than normal. And I mean that in every loving way possible."

Ally closed her eyes, letting out a long sigh. "No, not really. You know that promotion I've been working my butt off for? The one my boss keeps promising me? Well, it went to someone else!" She said with a slight edge in her voice.

"Oh, honey, I'm so sorry! That totally sucks. I know you've been waiting for this for some time now."

"That's not even the worst part!" Ally practically yelled. "The promotion went to a guy. A guy younger than me, who basically just started out at the office, and who knows absolutely nothing. No experience. I have years of it. Years!" She slumped down further into the couch. "So unfair."

"That *is* unfair," Stephanie said, moving to put her arms around her friend to console her. "This world can be so cruel if you're a woman."

Ally sat there, silently holding her head in her hands. She was trying not to cry. For months she had been told that the promotion was hers, so she happily took on all the extra shifts and heavy workload, certain that all her hard work was finally about to pay off.

Stephanie's phone buzzed on the coffee table, indicating an incoming message. She let go of Ally and leaned over to retrieve her phone. "It's from Lily!" She exclaimed, her face lighting up. "She just got into town and will be here until tomorrow." Lily was an old friend from college. The three of them were inseparable back then, they did everything together. That is, until Lily fell in love and moved away to be with the guy. It was the first time they had all been apart. The three of them were so close they considered each other their sister.

Ally tried to smile, but her face just refused to cooperate. She just wasn't feeling the excitement that her friend did right now.

"Oh, she sent a picture." Stephanie said, clicking on the attachment Lily had sent her. When it loaded her hand flew to her mouth. "O.M.G." she said in a squeaky voice. "It's a ring. They're engaged! Oh, it's about time for those two, don't ya think? I've never seen a couple more in love. And look at that rock- wow!"

Ally just sat there as her friend went on and on excitedly about the ring and engagement and everything. She knew she should be excited and happy for her friend, but it only made her feel worse. And that fact made her feel like she was being a horrible friend. She loved Lily, she really did. She was one of the best friends she had ever had, besides Stephanie, and she deserved this. But Ally couldn't help feeling like she had a weight tied to her ankles, dragging her down to the darkest depths as everyone around her flourished and succeeded.

Stephanie's phone chimed again, this time with an incoming video call. She scooted as close as she could to Ally, practically sitting on her lap, and answered the call.

"Well, hello you two beautiful creatures." Lily said once her face appeared on the screen.

Ally put on her best fake smile as Stephanie screeched onto the speaker. "Ahh! How are you? You look so, so good. Being engaged totally agrees with you. And I am absolutely jealous by the way," she added. Stephanie always rambled on and talked really fast when she was excited. She was hard to keep up with when that happened.

Lily laughed. "I am doing amazing. Obviously," she said with a smile as she rolled her eyes.

"Well, it's about time, girl. I was beginning to think you two would never tie the knot,"

Ally blinked hard, just realizing that she had totally

spaced out for most of the conversation. "I am so happy for you," she offered weakly. It wasn't much, but she figured she should at least contribute something to the conversation. She didn't want to somehow accidentally offend her friend on her big day. She had every right to be over-the-moon excited, it was her time. So Ally did her best to put on a happy face for her friend.

"Aw, thanks hun. What about you? I haven't heard much news from your end lately. How's the promotion going? You got it, right?" Lily asked cheerfully.

Well, that didn't last long.

Stephanie looked at Ally with a look that said "I'm sorry."

Ally turned back to the screen and puffed out a heavy sigh. "Actually . . no," she admitted, the weight tying itself back on. "I was passed over. Again." Stephanie took control of the conversation, turning the screen towards herself. "Our poor girl did all the work, plus tons extra, and they went ahead and gave it to a man, as usual," she scoffed.

"Oh, sweetie, I am so sorry. Not what you wanted, huh? And here I am blasting my good news, rubbing it in your face. Some friend I am."

"You didn't know."

"Still." Lily tapped her chin thoughtfully. "Hey,

why don't we all go out tonight? We can dance, have some drinks, forget all about those damn men at the office. What do you say? And maybe celebrate a little?" She asked, waving her hand around so the diamond flashed across the screen. It really was an impressive rock.

"I don't know, guys," Ally admitted, looking at both of them. "I really am so happy for you, Lil. I just, I'm really not in a party mood. You can go though," she offered, putting her hand on Stephanie's arm. "The two of you dance the night away and celebrate. I just can't. Not tonight." She felt horrible for missing her friend's celebration, but she couldn't bring herself to fake happiness for very long. She would have just an absolutely miserable time and bring down the mood. "I promise Lily, I will make this up to you. I'll even fly out to see you this time if I have to."

Her friend thought about it for a minute. "I suppose, but you owe me. Big time." She winked.

Ally left the two of them to plan out their night and retreated to her room. She took out her laptop and sat on her bed with it. She's been thinking about possibly searching for a different job, on the off chance the promotion didn't actually go through. She couldn't think of a single reason not to now, so she set off searching for job openings in their area. At this point, she didn't even care if the job was in her field or not.

Stephanie knocked on her door before poking her head in. "I'm about to head out, are you sure I can't tempt you into joining?" She asked, pouting her lips.

Ally laughed. "I'm sure. I wouldn't be any fun at all. I'd probably just end up sulking in the corner or something."

"Aw, that's too bad. Well, just try not to think about the negative things too much, okay? And I promise to check on you throughout the night."

"Totally not necessary, but thanks." Ally said, smiling at her friend. "Have a great time tonight and tell Lily I said 'I'm sorry and congratulations.'"

"Will do. Later, sweetie." Stephanie waved as she headed out the door.

Ally couldn't help feeling bad. She hadn't seen her friend in a long time. She shook her head, trying to lose the negative thoughts, and continued on her job search.

After a couple hours Ally was beginning to feel a little sleepy. She was about to shut her laptop down when a pop-up ad for a tropical resort caught her eye. Maybe that's just what I need, she thought to herself. Just get away from everything and everyone for a while. She abandoned any thought of job searches and began looking up prices and destinations instead. Ally was never one to put herself first. It's time, she thought. It's finally my time. So before getting some sleep and losing her new found confidence, she booked herself a week-long tropical getaway.

Sighing with contentment, Ally closed her laptop and went to bed, dreaming of white sand and margaritas.

Two

"HOW WAS LAST NIGHT?" Ally asked Stephanie as she put the ingredients together for her morning protein shake.

"It was. . . a blur," she answered, not quite fully awake yet.

Ally smiled as she chopped up her fruit and added it to the blender. To her it looked like they may have overdone it a little, making her feel better about having missed last night. She preferred not to wake up with a hangover. She was getting a little too old for that.

Warning Stephanie to cover her ears, Ally started up the blender. "Woah, who started up the construction site in here?" Lily yelled over the noise as she stumbled out of Stephanie's bedroom. "It's way too early for that, girl."

"Oh yeah, Lily spent the night here last night so you could see each other before she went back home." Stephanie laughed. "I almost forgot."

The two girls wrapped their arms around each other. "I am so sorry I missed the celebration." Ally said, making sure to keep her voice at a whisper.

"That is all right, hun. I totally understand. And. . . I don't really remember too much, but I'm sure you didn't miss anything too exciting,' she said as she slid onto the couch next to Stephanie. "Who let me drink so much, anyway?"

Laughing, Ally handed her hungover friends each a glass. "Here, drink this. I'm sure it'll help. I'll go get you two some aspirin as well."

"Is this supposed to be healthy? Because it tastes amazing, which means it can't be healthy," Lily said, taking a big gulp. "I really should start making these for myself. Can you write down the recipe for me, pretty please?" She asked while batting her long eyelashes.

Ally handed them their aspirin. "Sure thing."

"This should help get me in shape in time for my wedding, right? Which you both are coming to. . . as bridesmaids?" She asked hopefully, looking between the two of them.

"Of course!"

"Absolutely!" High pitched screams filled the apartment, despite the hangovers they were experiencing.

"I love you girls." Lily said as they embraced in a group hug. "I wouldn't be able to do the wedding without the two of you."

"Aw. We love you too, Lil. And we wouldn't miss it for the world."

The three girls talked for a few hours more. It was as if they had never been apart. Finally, Lily stood up. "I really hate this, but I do have a plane to catch. I'm going to miss you girls."

"We'll miss you too."

"How about I call you tomorrow sometime and we can set up a schedule to video chat so we can start some wedding planning?"

"I'm in!" Stephanie replied.

They both looked to Ally, who hadn't said anything in some time. "Um, actually," she said, looking down at her feet, "I'm leaving tomorrow."

"What?!" They both yelled in unison. Stephanie looked at her friend with concern in her eyes. "What do you mean, leaving? Where are you going? Is everything alright?"

"Everything's fine," Ally reassured them. "I just

need to get away from everything for a while. Focus on me a bit, clear my head."

Lily nodded. "I totally get that. You've worked so hard, you really deserve it. You go, have fun, and destress."

"It'll be good for you," Stephanie agreed.

Ally took her friend's hands. "I can still video call from the resort though. I'll make time for you, promise. We'll help give you the magical fairytale wedding of your dreams."

"Deal," Lily said. They said their goodbyes and she was off again.

Three

ALLY SAT in her window seat of the plane, and took a deep breath. Suddenly she wasn't sure she could do this. Being away from everyone, and alone, for an entire week? What was she thinking? No, she told herself. You are a grown woman, you need to do this. You need this. After the way she was mistreated at work for so long, she really did.

The whole ride to the resort she held the inner debate with herself. She wasn't fully confident that she had made the right decision until she stepped off the plane, and was hit with a warm ocean breeze. Salt clung in the air and palm trees lined the streets wherever she went. It was nothing like back home. Ally instantly felt at peace.

Feeling lighter on her feet, Ally headed in the direction of her resort. Her home for the next week. She took in the sights and the sounds. The heavenly smells. She practically bounced up to the front desk to check in, a huge smile taking over her face. After checking in she headed up to her room, key in one hand, maps of fun tourist-like destinations within walking distance of the resort and event schedules in the other. There was so much to see and do here. Ally wondered how much she'd actually get to do while she was here.

Hwe room was unlike any other room she's stayed in before. The bed was huge, covered in decorative pillows with patterns of coral and various fish on them. The mirror hanging on the wall was adorned in seashells and starfish. The pull cord on the ceiling fan also held a small starfish at the end, Starfish was the theme of her room, she concluded. And she loved it. One entire wall was actually huge sliding glass doors that led onto a balcony. She walked out, and the scene before her was absolutely breathtaking. More palm trees lined a white sand beach, and the sun reflected off the crystal blue water, making it shimmer. I never want to go home, Ally suddenly thought to herself.

She made quick calls to her friends to let them know she made it safely and to brag a little bit about everything she'd seen and experienced so far.. Let's face it, she didn't have much in her life to brag about, so she enjoyed every minute of it, including the jealousy in her friends' voices.

After a quick change of clothes she headed down to search for some dinner and then to explore the beach a bit. She was delighted to discover several bars and small restaurants sat directly on the beach. She wasn't going to need those event brochures after all, she smiled to herself.

Ally chose a restaurant that resembled a giant grass hut. The tables were situated under giant umbrellas and had a great view of the ocean and a small stage where musicians played nightly. She didn't go to many concerts at all back home. She promised herself that she'd at least catch a couple performances while down here. She wanted to get in as many new experiences as she could. Who knows when she'd ever get another opportunity like this.

The tables around her started filling up with couples, leaving her the only single person, but Ally didn't care. She happily munched on her burger and fries, which to her, was the best burger she'd ever eaten. She took her time, enjoying not only the mouth watering food, but the whole atmosphere. It was easy to forget life's stresses here, and the whole promotion ordeal slipped out of her mind, blowing away on the light evening breeze.

Full from the delicious meal, Ally decided to take a walk on the beach. She passed several groups of people who were either drinking, playing music, or splashing around in the water. Shoes in hand, she walked along the water's edge, letting it wash over her feet. Even the water felt warm and comforting.

THE NEXT MORNING when Ally woke up, she felt better than she had in a long time. She couldn't remember the last time she slept through the entire night, let alone woke up feeling refreshed. She'd never slept in a bed this fluffy before either. It was like sleeping on a cloud. Ally stretched, but made no move to leave her cloud bed. Only when her stomach rumbled loudly did she actually feel the need to get up.

The breakfast buffet held more food than she'd ever seen in one place. Her eyes went straight to the selection of fresh fruit. Finding a bowl, she filled it with strawberries, raspberries, blackberries, kiwi, mango, and some sweet grapes. There was nothing better than a nice fruit salad.

As she popped a couple raspberries in her mouth a

man approached her table. "Pardon me for asking, but did I see you at the show last night? Down by the beach?

Ally chewed quickly so she could answer him. What could be more embarrassing than choking right now? "I was, yes. I really enjoyed it." She looked up at the man and her heart nearly skipped a beat. Standing in front of her was, in her mind, the sexiest man alive. He was tall, broad shoulders, brown, windswept hair, and piercing blue eyes.

"Wait," she said, "you were one of the guitarists, weren't you? You played near the end of the night."

The man chuckled. "That was me, yes. I'm Darren," he said, holding out his hand.

"You were great," Ally said, taking his hand. "Your playing, I mean. I'm Ally."

"A pleasure to meet you, Ally. I hope you don't mind me asking, but have you come here alone? I only ask because last night I noticed you were the only single person. You kind of stood out, but in a good way." He gave her a warm, friendly smile, hoping his question didn't come off too stalkerish. When he noticed her in the crowd last night he was instantly drawn to her. He could feel from his place up on the stage that there was something special about this woman. He couldn't get her off his mind, and he knew he just had to get to know her.

Ally wasn't sure if she should really tell a stranger that she had in fact, come alone. That she was hours and hours as well as many miles away from anyone she knew. But she liked him. Something about Darren told her he could be trusted. It was his eyes, they were kind, and caring. Ally cleared her throat. "I did. I just wanted to get away from it all for a while."

"Well, I hope you're going to be sticking around here for a while?" He asked with a hopeful glint in his eye.

"All week." Ally admitted.

"That's great," Darren smiled brightly. "Listen, I've got to run, but perhaps one of these nights I can join you for dinner? No one should be alone. And I'm playing a lunch show down by the beach today, in case you're interested," he said before taking off.

Ally watched as he disappeared to another part of the resort. Weird, she thought. Although, attention from a sexy guitar player is always nice. Not that she had much experience with that. She decided she would go check out Darren's set later. Until then she wandered around, checking out the local shops. Her friends would appreciate small gifts, especially Lily. Maybe she could find something fun and unique for Lily for a wedding present. While browsing the shelves of locally made items, Ally's thoughts kept drifting back to the sexy guitar player. At some point, pretty much every girl dreams of being with a musician. Ally was no exception. She was starting to get excited about seeing him play.

Back at the resort, she carefully packed away the treasures that she had purchased. She couldn't wait to see the looks on her friends' faces when she presented them with their gifts. She loved buying things for other people. Noting the time, Ally hopped in for a quick shower and took longer than normal to pick out an outfit for lunch. She wanted something that would catch Darren's eye, but at the same time allow her skin to breathe, and keep her from sweating too much and becoming a gross mess. No one wants that.

Five

THE BEACH WAS BUSIER than it was last night. All the tables in the area around the stage were already pretty much filled. Ally decided to grab something small to eat and stand up near the stage. She hoped that Darren would be able to find her. Not that he was going to be searching for her. But a girl can hope, right?

There were only two acts playing during lunch. Darren was playing the second half. When he stepped out onto the stage Ally noticed all the girls yelling and screaming, trying to get his attention. Heat crept up in her cheeks as she began to feel jealousy tug at her. She had to remind herself that he wasn't hers. But Darren scanned the crowd, smiling wide when he finally spotted her. Ally returned his smile and as his set went on, she felt herself feeling a little giddy.

After the ending note of Darren's last song floated over the crowd, Ally found herself yelling and cheering with everyone else. To her surprise, Darren set his guitar down and walked through the sea of people, straight for her. She pretended not to see the jealous stares of the women nearby.

"What is this for?" She asked as Darren handed her a sunflower.

"I saw this and its beauty reminded me of you," he said, making her blush even more. "And there were sunflowers on the shirt you wore last night. Again, reminding me of you."

"Thank you," Ally said as she accepted the flower. It was such a beautiful and romantic gesture, nothing like she's experienced so far in the dating world. She didn't have the best track record when it came to men. "You were great again, by the way," she told him. "I could listen to you sing and play for hours."

"That's what every musician loves to hear," he laughed. "Are you busy today? I was thinking we could maybe go on a hike together. Just the two of us." His eyes sparkled. "I know of a great trail that leads up to a waterfall. I think you'd really like it."

Ally loved that idea. "That sounds amazing," she beamed at him.

He rubbed his hands together. "Great. How about we both go get changed and I'll meet you in the lobby of your resort?"

Ally nodded.

Looking down at the sandals she was currently wearing, he laughed. "You have some type of shoe suitable for hiking, right?"

"I'm sure I have something that will work."

"Excellent," he said. "See you soon." He left to go pack up his guitar and change, but not before planting a delicate kiss on her forehead.

Ally practically swooned. This was definitely something that she could get used to.

She rummaged through her bags, glad she packed her walking shoes at the last second. She usually lived in heels. Those, and sandals when not at work. Ally grabbed those, and changed into a comfortable pair of shorts with a loose fitting tank top. Remembering the waterfall that was supposed to be at the end of the hike, she decided to throw on a bikini under everything. Throwing her hair into a ponytail, she decided she was ready, and headed to what she was sure was her first date in many, many more years than she cared to admit.

Six

THE HIKING TRAIL that Darren chose took them through a forest filled with friendly little creatures and beautiful blooming flowers of all shapes and colors. Their sweet fragrance filled the air, and Ally breathed it all in. There wasn't much in the way of conversation as they made their way to the waterfall. The trail wasn't made for two people to walk side by side, forcing them to walk single file. Ally didn't mind though, the scenery was beautiful and she enjoyed being able to just look at it all, taking everything in. She wasn't being interrupted by questions or having to make small talk or anything.

Darren turned to look back at Ally after a while. "We're almost there," he said. "Promise," and flashed her a smile that gave her butterflies.

She listened closely, expecting to hear the thundering sounds you'd expect a waterfall to have. She didn't hear anything though, making her wonder how close they really were.

The trees suddenly gave way to a small lake. The waterfall flowing into it was super quiet, considering its size. Ally could easily see why people would love to come up here to swim. The two of them set their stuff down, dipping their feet in the water as they talked and got to know just about everything there was to know about each other. Ally found Darren incredibly easy to talk to, and she didn't open up to that many people.

They talked and swam, the cool waters refreshing after the hike. Ally floated on her back, feeling more relaxed than ever. It felt as if they were the only two people alive.

"Should we start heading back?" Darren asked as Ally dried her hair the best she could. She ran her fingers through it to remove any tangles. She didn't really want to leave, she thought she could stay here forever, but she reluctantly agreed. "I guess it did get kind of late on us, huh?" She laughed.

"It sure did," he agreed. "And I still owe you dinner, by the way," he said with a wink. "Would you like to have dinner with me now, or are you sick of me already?" he teased.

"Dinner sounds fantastic,"she said, and meant it. All that walking they did today has left her starving. "And I doubt that I could ever get sick of you."

By the time they arrived back at the beach, the sun had completely dried their clothing, so they chose to go straight to get something to eat. "This is my favorite spot," Darren said as they entered a small restaurant, named Fred's. He greeted everyone inside either with a friendly hug or a slap on the back. It seemed as if he was well loved around here. Ally suddenly felt almost like a groupie, the thought making her laugh on the inside.

He brought Ally over to a loud, smiling man who had an impressive tan. "This here," he said, slapping the man on his chest, " is Fred. The owner here. He's also kind of my best friend."

"On account of him eating here just about every day," the man joked, picking Darren up in a bear hug. He turned to Ally. "And who is this magnificent creature?" He asked, kissing her hand and doing a little bow.

Ally giggled, her cheeks bright red.

"This is Ally, we met right here on the beach. She's staying up at the resort just beyond the stage. She's alright," he said, shrugging his shoulders. "I guess." That sent the three of them laughing. Besides Lily and

Stephanie back home, Ally didn't have that many friends. But she really liked Fred. And she liked his friendship with Darren.

"Why don't you two go take a seat and I'll bring three specials?" Fred suggested, already heading into the kitchen.

"Three?" Ally asked Darren with a raised eyebrow and a playful smile.

"What can I say?" He shrugged. "Fred likes to invite himself along sometimes. Is that okay? I can always tell him to go away."

Ally laughed. "No, it's perfectly all right. He's your friend. And this is his place, after all."

Apparently the special was actually a table filled with many different types of food. You name it, it was there. The three of them ate, shared stories, and just had a great time. Ally felt as if she had known these two her whole life.

After eating all they could, Darren and Ally said goodbye to Fred, promising to come by again. "I like her," he told Darren. Find a way to hold onto this one."

Returning to the beach, they sat close to the water's edge, listening to the sounds of the waves. The sun was setting, and it looked like a painting up in the sky. Ally didn't think she'd ever seen so many colors.

Feeling his eyes on her, Ally turned to face Darren. He gently took her head in his hands, and he leaned in for their very first kiss. As soon as his lips touched hers, she felt electricity throughout her entire body. He had kept the kiss light, but it left her wanting more.

After watching the sunset laying in his arms, Darren walked her back to her resort, neither one wanting the night to end.

"O.M.G. TELL ME EVERYTHING!" Stephanie exclaimed when Ally called her that night. Ally sighed. "He's the most amazing man ever-smart, sexy, caring, romantic, and he's a musician!"

"Girl, I am so jealous! Sounds like you made a good choice going down there. I'm happy for you. But just promise me you'll be careful."

Ally's face hurt from smiling so much. "I sure did. I'll call you tomorrow and fill you in some more. Goodnight, I miss you."

Ally went to sleep that night knowing she was falling in love. She knew it maybe wasn't the smartest idea, considering she was leaving in a few days. She pushed the thought away, she was determined to enjoy every minute that she had with Darren.

* * *

Every morning since they met Darren would be waiting for Ally in the lobby of her resort, and he always had a single sunflower for her. She kept them in a cup of water in her room.

He showed her around town, brought her to all his favorite places, and all the hidden hot spots. They even went up to the waterfall a couple more times, just to have some time with just the two of them.

When Darren had a show Ally was always front row, cheering him on. After each song he would lean down for a quick kiss, and she didn't care if anyone was watching them.

As promised, they went down to Fred's for lunch, and it felt like they were all old friends. He would always greet Ally with a warm hug, and try to feed her everything under the sun. That man sure loved to cook.

Neither of them wanted the week to end. The more they got to know each other the deeper they fell. Every minute that they had free, was spent together.

On her last night there, Ally nearly broke down. This man was everything she'd ever wanted, everything she'd hoped for, and in a matter of hours now, she'd be leaving him. She could feel her heart beginning to break.

There was a huge party happening on the beach, and Darren convinced Ally to go with him. The two lovebirds sat cuddled up next to the bonfire, just enjoying each other's company.

"I bought you a present," Darren whispered in her ear. "Just a little something so you won't forget me." He shifted a little and pulled a small box out of his pants pocket. Inside was a necklace, with a pendant in the shape of a sunflower, just like the ones he brought her every morning. Ally teared up as he fastened it around her neck.

"It's perfect," she told him, and kissed him fiercely. "I love it."

The next morning Ally headed to the airport for the long trip home. As she sat in the terminal waiting to board, she took out her phone and called Lily. It went straight to voicemail. She rolled her eyes and left a message, telling her friend that she had the most amazing time and was on her way home. She ended the call by telling her friend that she would see her soon and that she finally had a date for her wedding, and that she would meet him very soon.

She hung up the phone, looked over to Darren, sitting next to her. She smiled as their flight was called. They walked hand in hand to the gate, ready to start the next chapter of their adventure.